Samuel Langhorne Clemens (November 30, 1835 – April 21, 1910), known by his pen name Mark Twain, was an American writer, humorist, entrepreneur, publisher, and lecturer. He was lauded as the "greatest humorist this country has produced", and William Faulkner called him "the father of American literature". His novels include The Adventures of Tom Sawyer (1876) and its sequel, the Adventures of Huckleberry Finn (1884), the latter often called "The Great American Novel".

Twain was raised in Hannibal, Missouri, which later provided the setting for Tom Sawyer and Huckleberry Finn. He served an apprenticeship with a printer and then worked as a typesetter, contributing articles to the newspaper of his older brother Orion Clemens. He later became a riverboat pilot on the Mississippi River before heading west to join Orion in Nevada. (Source: Wikipedia)

Literary works:

The Gilded Age: A Tale of Today (1873)
The Prince and the Pauper (1881)
A Connecticut Yankee in
King Arthur's Court (1889)
The American Claimant (1892)
Pudd'nhead Wilson (1894)
Personal Recollections of Joan of Arc (1896)
A Horse's Tale (1907)
The Mysterious Stranger (1916, posthumous)
The Adventures of Tom Sawyer (1876)
Adventures of Huckleberry Finn (1884)
Tom Sawyer Abroad (1894)
Tom Sawyer, Detective (1896)
"Eve's Diary" (1906)

A Dog's Tale

MARK TWAIN

PRINCE CLASSICS

PRINCE CLASSICS

This is a work of fiction. Names, characters, places, and incidents either are the product of the author's imagination or are used fictitiously. Any resemblance to actual persons, living or dead, events, or locales is entirely coincidental.

First Printing: 2020

ISBN 978-93-89682-02-1 (paperback)

ISBN 978-93-89682-03-8 (Hardcover)

Published by Prince Classics

www.princeclassics.com

Contents

A Dog's Tale

CHAPTER I.

My father was a St. Bernard, my mother was a collie, but I am a Presbyterian. This is what my mother told me, I do not know these nice distinctions myself. To me they are only fine large words meaning nothing. My mother had a fondness for such; she liked to say them, and see other dogs look surprised and envious, as wondering how she got so much education. But, indeed, it was not real education; it was only show: she got the words by listening in the dining-room and drawing-room when there was company, and by going with the children to Sunday-school and listening there; and whenever she heard a large word she said it over to herself many times, and so was able to keep it until there was a dogmatic gathering in the neighborhood, then she would get it off, and surprise and distress them all, from pocket-pup to mastiff, which rewarded her for all her trouble. If there was a stranger he was nearly sure to be suspicious, and when he got his breath again he would ask her what it meant. And she always told him. He was never expecting this but thought he would catch her; so when she told him, he was the one that looked ashamed, whereas he had thought it was going to be she. The others were always waiting for this, and glad of it and proud of her, for they knew what was going to happen, because they had had experience. When she told the meaning of a big word they were all so taken up with admiration that it never occurred to any dog to doubt if it was the right one; and that was natural, because, for one thing, she answered up so promptly that it seemed like a dictionary speaking, and for another thing, where could they find out whether it was right or not? for she was the only cultivated dog there was. By and by, when I was older, she brought home the word Unintellectual, one time, and worked it pretty hard all the week at different gatherings, making much unhappiness and despondency; and it was at this time that I noticed that during that week she was asked for the meaning at eight different assemblages, and flashed out a fresh definition every time, which showed me that she had more presence of mind than culture, though I said nothing, of course. She had one word which she always kept on hand, and ready, like a life-preserver, a kind of emergency word to strap on when she was likely to get washed overboard in a sudden way—that was the word Synonymous. When she happened to fetch out a long word which had had its day weeks before and its prepared meanings gone to her dump-pile, if there was a stranger there of course it knocked him groggy for a couple of minutes, then he would come to, and by that time she would be away down wind on another tack, and not expecting anything; so when he'd hail and ask her to cash in, I (the only dog on the inside of her game) could see her canvas flicker a moment—but only just a moment—then it would belly out taut and full, and she would say, as calm as a summer's day, "It's synonymous with supererogation," or some godless long reptile of a word like that, and go placidly about and skim away on the next tack, perfectly comfortable, you know, and leave that stranger looking profane and embarrassed, and the initiated slatting the floor with their tails in unison and their faces transfigured with a holy joy.

And it was the same with phrases. She would drag home a whole phrase, if it had a grand sound, and play it six nights and two matinees, and explain it a new way every time—which she had to, for all she cared for was the phrase; she wasn't interested in what it meant, and knew those dogs hadn't wit enough to catch her, anyway. Yes, she was a daisy! She got so she wasn't afraid of anything, she had such confidence in the ignorance of those creatures. She even brought anecdotes that she had heard the family and the dinner-guests laugh and shout over; and as a rule she got the nub of one chestnut hitched onto another chestnut, where, of course, it didn't fit and hadn't any point; and when she delivered the nub she fell over and rolled on the floor and laughed and barked in the most insane way, while I could see that she was wondering to herself why it didn't seem as funny as it did when she first heard it. But no harm was done; the others rolled and barked too, privately ashamed of themselves for not seeing the point, and never suspecting that the fault was not with them and there wasn't any to see.

You can see by these things that she was of a rather vain and frivolous character; still, she had virtues, and enough to make up, I think. She had a kind heart and gentle ways, and never harbored resentments for injuries done her, but put them easily out of her mind and forgot them; and she taught her children her kindly way, and from her we learned also to be brave and prompt in time of danger, and not to run away, but face the peril that threatened friend or stranger, and help him the best we could without stopping to think what the cost might be to us. And she taught us not by words only, but by example, and that is the best way and the surest and the most lasting. Why, the brave things she did, the splendid things! she was just a soldier; and so modest about it—well, you couldn't help admiring her, and you couldn't help imitating her; not even a King Charles spaniel could remain entirely despicable in her society. So, as you see, there was more to her than her education.

CHAPTER II.

When I was well grown, at last, I was sold and taken away, and I never saw her again. She was broken-hearted, and so was I, and we cried; but she comforted me as well as she could, and said we were sent into this world for a wise and good purpose, and must do our duties without repining, take our life as we might find it, live it for the best good of others, and never mind about the results; they were not our affair. She said men who did like this would have a noble and beautiful reward by and by in another world, and although we animals would not go there, to do well and right without reward would give to our brief lives a worthiness and dignity which in itself would be a reward. She had gathered these things from time to time when she had gone to the Sunday-school with the children, and had laid them up in her memory more carefully than she had done with those other words and phrases; and she had studied them deeply, for her good and ours. One may see by this that she had a wise and thoughtful head, for all there was so much lightness and vanity in it.

So we said our farewells, and looked our last upon each other through our tears; and the last thing she said—keeping it for the last to make me remember it the better, I think—was, "In memory of me, when there is a time of danger to another do not think of yourself, think of your mother, and do as she would do."

Do you think I could forget that? No.

CHAPTER III.

It was such a charming home!—my new one; a fine great house, with pictures, and delicate decorations, and rich furniture, and no gloom anywhere, but all the wilderness of dainty colors lit up with flooding sunshine; and the spacious grounds around it, and the great garden—oh, greensward, and noble trees, and flowers, no end! And I was the same as a member of the family; and they loved me, and petted me, and did not give me a new name, but called me by my old one that was dear to me because my mother had given it me—Aileen Mavourneen. She got it out of a song; and the Grays knew that song, and said it was a beautiful name.

Mrs. Gray was thirty, and so sweet and so lovely, you cannot imagine it; and Sadie was ten, and just like her mother, just a darling slender little copy of her, with auburn tails down her back, and short frocks; and the baby was a year old, and plump and dimpled, and fond of me, and never could get enough of hauling on my tail, and hugging me, and laughing out its innocent happiness; and Mr. Gray was thirty-eight, and tall and slender and handsome, a little bald in front, alert, quick in his movements, business-like, prompt, decided, unsentimental, and with that kind of trim-chiseled face that just seems to glint and sparkle with frosty intellectuality! He was a renowned scientist. I do not know what the word means, but my mother would know how to use it and get effects. She would know how to depress a rat-terrier with it and make a lap-dog look sorry he came. But that is not the best one; the best one was Laboratory. My mother could organize a Trust on that one that would skin the tax-collars off the whole herd. The laboratory was not a book, or a picture, or a place to wash your hands in, as the college president's dog said—no, that is the lavatory; the laboratory is quite different, and is filled with jars, and bottles, and electrics, and wires, and strange machines; and every week other scientists came there and sat in the place, and used the machines, and discussed, and made what they called experiments and discoveries; and often I came, too, and stood around and listened, and tried to learn, for the sake of my mother, and in loving memory of her, although it was a pain to me, as realizing what she was losing out of her life and I gaining nothing at all; for try as I might, I was never able to make anything out of it at all.

Other times I lay on the floor in the mistress's work-room and slept, she gently using me for a foot-stool, knowing it pleased me, for it was a caress; other times I spent an hour in the nursery, and got well tousled and made happy; other times I watched by the crib there, when the baby was asleep and the nurse out for a few minutes on the baby's affairs; other times I romped and raced through the grounds and the garden with Sadie till we were tired out, then slumbered on the grass in the shade of a tree while she read her book; other times I went visiting among the neighbor dogs—for there were some most pleasant ones not far away, and one very handsome and courteous and graceful one, a curly-haired Irish setter by the name of Robin Adair, who was a Presbyterian like me, and belonged to the Scotch minister.

The servants in our house were all kind to me and were fond of me, and so, as you see, mine was a pleasant life. There could not be a happier dog that I was, nor a gratefuller one. I will say this for myself, for it is only the truth: I tried in all ways to do well and right, and honor my mother's memory and her teachings, and earn the happiness that had come to me, as best I could.

By and by came my little puppy, and then my cup was full, my happiness was perfect. It was the dearest little waddling thing, and so smooth and soft and velvety, and had such cunning little awkward paws, and such affectionate eyes, and such a sweet and innocent face; and it made me so proud to see how the children and their mother adored it, and fondled it, and exclaimed over every little wonderful thing it did. It did seem to me that life was just too lovely to—

Then came the winter. One day I was standing a watch in the nursery. That is to say, I was asleep on the bed. The baby was asleep in the crib, which was alongside the bed, on the side next the fireplace. It was the kind of crib that has a lofty tent over it made of gauzy stuff that you can see through. The nurse was out, and we two sleepers were alone. A spark from the wood-fire was shot out, and it lit on the slope of the tent. I suppose a quiet interval followed, then a scream from the baby awoke me, and there was that tent flaming up toward the ceiling! Before I could think, I sprang to the floor in my fright, and in a second was half-way to the door; but in the next half-second my mother's farewell was sounding in my ears, and I was back on the bed again. I reached my head through the flames and dragged the baby out by the waist-band, and tugged it along, and we fell to the floor together in a cloud of smoke; I snatched a new hold, and dragged the screaming little creature along and out at the door and around the bend of the hall, and was still tugging away, all excited and happy and proud, when the master's voice shouted:

"Begone you cursed beast!" and I jumped to save myself; but he was furiously quick, and chased me up, striking furiously at me with his cane, I dodging this way and that, in terror, and at last a strong blow fell upon my left foreleg, which made me shriek and fall, for the moment, helpless; the cane went up for another blow, but never descended, for the nurse's voice rang wildly out, "The nursery's on fire!" and the master rushed away in that direction, and my other bones were saved.

The pain was cruel, but, no matter, I must not lose any time; he might come back at any moment; so I limped on three legs to the other end of the hall, where there was a dark little stairway leading up into a garret where old boxes and such things were kept, as I had heard say, and where people seldom went. I managed to climb up there, then I searched my way through the dark among the piles of things, and hid in the secretest place I could find. It was foolish to be afraid there, yet still I was; so afraid that I held in and hardly even whimpered, though it would have been such a comfort to whimper, because that eases the pain, you know. But I could lick my leg, and that did some good.

For half an hour there was a commotion downstairs, and shoutings, and rushing footsteps, and then there was quiet again. Quiet for some minutes, and that was grateful to my spirit, for then my fears began to go down; and fears are worse than pains—oh, much worse. Then came a sound that froze me. They were calling me—calling me by name—hunting for me!

It was muffled by distance, but that could not take the terror out of it, and it was the most dreadful sound to me that I had ever heard. It went all about, everywhere, down there: along the halls, through all the rooms, in both stories, and in the basement and the cellar; then outside, and farther and farther away—then back, and all about the house again, and I thought it would never, never stop. But at last it did, hours and hours after the vague twilight of the garret had long ago been blotted out by black darkness.

Then in that blessed stillness my terrors fell little by little away, and I was at peace and slept. It was a good rest I had, but I woke before the twilight had come again. I was feeling fairly comfortable, and I could think out a plan now. I made a very good one; which was, to creep down, all the way down the back stairs, and hide behind the cellar door, and slip out and escape when the iceman came at dawn, while he was inside filling the refrigerator; then I would hide all day, and start on my journey when night came; my journey to—well, anywhere where they would not know me and betray me to the master. I was feeling almost cheerful now; then suddenly I thought: Why, what would life be without my puppy!

That was despair. There was no plan for me; I saw that; I must stay where I was; stay, and wait, and take what might come—it was not my affair; that was what life is—my mother had said it. Then—well, then the calling began again! All my sorrows came back. I said to myself, the master will never forgive. I did not know what I had done to make him so bitter and so unforgiving, yet I judged it was something a dog could not understand, but which was clear to a man and dreadful.

They called and called—days and nights, it seemed to me. So long that the hunger and thirst near drove me mad, and I recognized that I was getting very weak. When you are this way you sleep a great deal, and I did. Once I woke in an awful fright—it seemed to me that the calling was right there in the garret! And so it was: it was Sadie's voice, and she was crying; my name was falling from her lips all broken, poor thing, and I could not believe my ears for the joy of it when I heard her say:

"Come back to us—oh, come back to us, and forgive—it is all so sad without our—"

I broke in with SUCH a grateful little yelp, and the next moment Sadie was plunging and stumbling through the darkness and the lumber and shouting for the family to hear, "She's found, she's found!"

The days that followed—well, they were wonderful. The mother and Sadie and the servants—why, they just seemed to worship me. They couldn't seem to make me a bed that was fine enough; and as for food, they couldn't be satisfied with anything but game and delicacies that were out of season; and every day the friends and neighbors flocked in to hear about my heroism—that was the name they called it by, and it means agriculture. I remember my mother pulling it on a kennel once, and explaining it in that way, but didn't say what agriculture was, except that it was synonymous with intramural incandescence; and a dozen times a day Mrs. Gray and Sadie would tell the tale to new-comers, and say I risked my life to save the baby's, and both of us had burns to prove it, and then the company would pass me around and pet me and exclaim about me, and you could see the pride in the eyes of Sadie and her mother; and when the people wanted to know what made me limp, they looked ashamed and changed the subject, and sometimes when people hunted them this way and that way with questions about it, it looked to me as if they were going to cry.

And this was not all the glory; no, the master's friends came, a whole twenty of the most distinguished people, and had me in the laboratory, and discussed me as if I was a kind of discovery; and some of them said it was wonderful in a dumb beast, the finest exhibition of instinct they could call to mind; but the master said, with vehemence, "It's far above instinct; it's REASON, and many a man, privileged to be saved and go with you and me to a better world by right of its possession, has less of it that this poor silly quadruped that's foreordained to perish;" and then he laughed, and said: "Why, look at me—I'm a sarcasm! bless you, with all my grand intelligence, the only thing I inferred was that the dog had gone mad and was destroying the child, whereas but for the beast's intelligence—it's REASON, I tell you!—the child would have perished!"

They disputed and disputed, and I was the very center of subject of it all, and I wished my mother could know that this grand honor had come to me;

it would have made her proud.

Then they discussed optics, as they called it, and whether a certain injury to the brain would produce blindness or not, but they could not agree about it, and said they must test it by experiment by and by; and next they discussed plants, and that interested me, because in the summer Sadie and I had planted seeds—I helped her dig the holes, you know—and after days and days a little shrub or a flower came up there, and it was a wonder how that could happen; but it did, and I wished I could talk—I would have told those people about it and shown then how much I knew, and been all alive with the subject; but I didn't care for the optics; it was dull, and when they came back to it again it bored me, and I went to sleep.

Pretty soon it was spring, and sunny and pleasant and lovely, and the sweet mother and the children patted me and the puppy good-by, and went away on a journey and a visit to their kin, and the master wasn't any company for us, but we played together and had good times, and the servants were kind and friendly, so we got along quite happily and counted the days and waited for the family.

And one day those men came again, and said, now for the test, and they took the puppy to the laboratory, and I limped three-leggedly along, too, feeling proud, for any attention shown to the puppy was a pleasure to me, of course. They discussed and experimented, and then suddenly the puppy shrieked, and they set him on the floor, and he went staggering around, with his head all bloody, and the master clapped his hands and shouted:

"There, I've won—confess it! He's as blind as a bat!"

And they all said:

"It's so—you've proved your theory, and suffering humanity owes you a great debt from henceforth," and they crowded around him, and wrung his hand cordially and thankfully, and praised him.

But I hardly saw or heard these things, for I ran at once to my little darling, and snuggled close to it where it lay, and licked the blood, and it put its head against mine, whimpering softly, and I knew in my heart it was a comfort to it in its pain and trouble to feel its mother's touch, though it could not see me. Then it dropped down, presently, and its little velvet nose rested upon the floor, and it was still, and did not move any more.

Soon the master stopped discussing a moment, and rang in the footman, and said, "Bury it in the far corner of the garden," and then went on with the discussion, and I trotted after the footman, very happy and grateful, for I knew the puppy was out of its pain now, because it was asleep. We went far down the garden to the farthest end, where the children and the nurse and the puppy and I used to play in the summer in the shade of a great elm, and there the footman dug a hole, and I saw he was going to plant the puppy, and I was glad, because it would grow and come up a fine handsome dog, like Robin Adair, and be a beautiful surprise for the family when they came home; so I tried to help him dig, but my lame leg was no good, being stiff, you know, and you have to have two, or it is no use. When the footman had finished and covered little Robin up, he patted my head, and there were tears in his eyes, and he said: "Poor little doggie, you saved HIS child!"

I have watched two whole weeks, and he doesn't come up! This last week a fright has been stealing upon me. I think there is something terrible about this. I do not know what it is, but the fear makes me sick, and I cannot eat, though the servants bring me the best of food; and they pet me so, and even come in the night, and cry, and say, "Poor doggie—do give it up and come home; don't break our hearts!" and all this terrifies me the more, and makes me sure something has happened. And I am so weak; since yesterday I cannot stand on my feet anymore. And within this hour the servants, looking toward the sun where it was sinking out of sight and the night chill coming on, said things I could not understand, but they carried something cold to my heart.

"Those poor creatures! They do not suspect. They will come home in the morning, and eagerly ask for the little doggie that did the brave deed, and who of us will be strong enough to say the truth to them: 'The humble little friend is gone where go the beasts that perish.'"

About Author

Samuel Langhorne Clemens (November 30, 1835 – April 21, 1910), known by his pen name Mark Twain, was an American writer, humorist, entrepreneur, publisher, and lecturer. He was lauded as the "greatest humorist this country has produced", and William Faulkner called him "the father of American literature". His novels include The Adventures of Tom Sawyer (1876) and its sequel, the Adventures of Huckleberry Finn (1884), the latter often called "The Great American Novel".

Twain was raised in Hannibal, Missouri, which later provided the setting for Tom Sawyer and Huckleberry Finn. He served an apprenticeship with a printer and then worked as a typesetter, contributing articles to the newspaper of his older brother Orion Clemens. He later became a riverboat pilot on the Mississippi River before heading west to join Orion in Nevada. He referred humorously to his lack of success at mining, turning to journalism for the Virginia City Territorial Enterprise. His humorous story, "The Celebrated Jumping Frog of Calaveras County", was published in 1865, based on a story that he heard at Angels Hotel in Angels Camp, California, where he had spent some time as a miner. The short story brought international attention and was even translated into French. His wit and satire, in prose and in speech, earned praise from critics and peers, and he was a friend to presidents, artists, industrialists, and European royalty.

Twain earned a great deal of money from his writings and lectures, but he invested in ventures that lost most of it—such as the Paige Compositor, a mechanical typesetter that failed because of its complexity and imprecision. He filed for bankruptcy in the wake of these financial setbacks, but he eventually overcame his financial troubles with the help of Henry Huttleston Rogers. He eventually paid all his creditors in full, even though his bankruptcy relieved him of having to do so.

Twain was born shortly after an appearance of Halley's Comet, and he predicted that he would "go out with it" as well; he died the day after the comet returned.

Biography

Early life

Samuel Langhorne Clemens was born on November 30, 1835, in Florida, Missouri, the sixth of seven children born to Jane (née Lampton; 1803–1890), a native of Kentucky, and John Marshall Clemens (1798–1847), a native of Virginia. His parents met when his father moved to Missouri, and they were married in 1823. Twain was of Cornish, English, and Scots-Irish descent. Only three of his siblings survived childhood: Orion (1825–1897), Henry (1838–1858), and Pamela (1827–1904). His sister Margaret (1830–1839) died when Twain was three, and his brother Benjamin (1832–1842) died three years later. His brother Pleasant Hannibal (1828) died at three weeks of age.

When he was four, Twain's family moved to Hannibal, Missouri, a port town on the Mississippi River that inspired the fictional town of St. Petersburg in The Adventures of Tom Sawyer and the Adventures of Huckleberry Finn. Slavery was legal in Missouri at the time, and it became a theme in these writings. His father was an attorney and judge, who died of pneumonia in 1847, when Twain was 11. The next year, Twain left school after the fifth grade to become a printer's apprentice. In 1851, he began working as a typesetter, contributing articles and humorous sketches to the Hannibal Journal, a newspaper that Orion owned. When he was 18, he left Hannibal and worked as a printer in New York City, Philadelphia, St. Louis, and Cincinnati, joining the newly formed International Typographical Union, the printers trade union. He educated himself in public libraries in the evenings, finding wider information than at a conventional school.

Twain describes his boyhood in Life on the Mississippi, stating that "there was but one permanent ambition" among his comrades: to be a steamboatman.

Pilot was the grandest position of all. The pilot, even in those days of trivial wages, had a princely salary – from a hundred and fifty to two hundred and fifty dollars a month, and no board to pay.

As Twain describes it, the pilot's prestige exceeded that of the captain. The pilot had to:

...get up a warm personal acquaintanceship with every old snag and one-limbed cottonwood and every obscure wood pile that ornaments the banks of this river for twelve hundred miles; and more than that, must... actually know where these things are in the dark

Steamboat pilot Horace E. Bixby took Twain on as a cub pilot to teach him the river between New Orleans and St. Louis for $500 (equivalent to $14,000 in 2018), payable out of Twain's first wages after graduating. Twain studied the Mississippi, learning its landmarks, how to navigate its currents effectively, and how to read the river and its constantly shifting channels, reefs, submerged snags, and rocks that would "tear the life out of the strongest vessel that ever floated". It was more than two years before he received his pilot's license. Piloting also gave him his pen name from "mark twain", the leadsman's cry for a measured river depth of two fathoms (12 feet), which was safe water for a steamboat.

As a young pilot, Clemens served on the steamer A. B. Chambers with Grant Marsh, who became famous for his exploits as a steamboat captain on the Missouri River. The two liked each other, and admired one another, and maintained a correspondence for many years after Clemens left the river.

While training, Samuel convinced his younger brother Henry to work with him, and even arranged a post of mud clerk for him on the steamboat Pennsylvania. On June 13, 1858, the steamboat's boiler exploded; Henry succumbed to his wounds on June 21. Twain claimed to have foreseen this death in a dream a month earlier, which inspired his interest in parapsychology; he was an early member of the Society for Psychical Research. Twain was guilt-stricken and held himself responsible for the rest of his life. He continued to work on the river and was a river pilot until the Civil War broke out in 1861, when traffic was curtailed along the Mississippi River. At the start of hostilities, he enlisted briefly in a local Confederate unit. He later wrote the sketch "The Private History of a Campaign That Failed", describing how he and his friends had been Confederate volunteers for two weeks before disbanding.

He then left for Nevada to work for his brother Orion, who was Secretary of the Nevada Territory. Twain describes the episode in his book Roughing It.

Travels

Orion became secretary to Nevada Territory governor James W. Nye in 1861, and Twain joined him when he moved west. The brothers traveled more than two weeks on a stagecoach across the Great Plains and the Rocky Mountains, visiting the Mormon community in Salt Lake City.

Twain's journey ended in the silver-mining town of Virginia City, Nevada, where he became a miner on the Comstock Lode. He failed as a miner and went to work at the Virginia City newspaper Territorial Enterprise, working under a friend, the writer Dan DeQuille. He first used his pen name here on February 3, 1863, when he wrote a humorous travel account entitled "Letter From Carson – re: Joe Goodman; party at Gov. Johnson's; music" and signed it "Mark Twain".

His experiences in the American West inspired Roughing It, written during 1870–71 and published in 1872. His experiences in Angels Camp (in Calaveras County, California) provided material for "The Celebrated Jumping Frog of Calaveras County" (1865).

Twain moved to San Francisco in 1864, still as a journalist, and met writers such as Bret Harte and Artemus Ward. He may have been romantically involved with the poet Ina Coolbrith.

His first success as a writer came when his humorous tall tale "The Celebrated Jumping Frog of Calaveras County" was published on November 18, 1865, in the New York weekly The Saturday Press, bringing him national attention. A year later, he traveled to the Sandwich Islands (present-day Hawaii) as a reporter for the Sacramento Union. His letters to the Union were popular and became the basis for his first lectures.

In 1867, a local newspaper funded his trip to the Mediterranean aboard the Quaker City, including a tour of Europe and the Middle East. He wrote a collection of travel letters which were later compiled as The Innocents Abroad (1869). It was on this trip that he met fellow passenger Charles Langdon, who showed him a picture of his sister Olivia. Twain later claimed to have fallen in love at first sight.

Upon returning to the United States, Twain was offered honorary membership in Yale University's secret society Scroll and Key in 1868. Its devotion to "fellowship, moral and literary self-improvement, and charity" suited him well.

Marriage and children

Twain and Olivia Langdon corresponded throughout 1868. She rejected his first marriage proposal, but they were married in Elmira, New York in February 1870, where he courted her and managed to overcome her father's initial reluctance. She came from a "wealthy but liberal family"; through her, he met abolitionists, "socialists, principled atheists and activists for women's rights and social equality", including Harriet Beecher Stowe (his next-door neighbor in Hartford, Connecticut), Frederick Douglass, and writer and utopian socialist William Dean Howells, who became a long-time friend. The couple lived in Buffalo, New York, from 1869 to 1871. He owned a stake in the Buffalo Express newspaper and worked as an editor and writer. While they were living in Buffalo, their son Langdon died of diphtheria at the age of 19 months. They had three daughters: Susy (1872–1896), Clara (1874–1962), and Jean (1880–1909).

Twain moved his family to Hartford, Connecticut, where he arranged the building of a home starting in 1873. In the 1870s and 1880s, the family summered at Quarry Farm in Elmira, the home of Olivia's sister, Susan Crane. In 1874, Susan had a study built apart from the main house so that Twain would have a quiet place in which to write. Also, he smoked cigars constantly, and Susan did not want him to do so in her house.

Twain wrote many of his classic novels during his 17 years in Hartford (1874–1891) and over 20 summers at Quarry Farm. They include The Adventures of Tom Sawyer (1876), The Prince and the Pauper (1881), Life on the Mississippi (1883), Adventures of Huckleberry Finn (1884), and A

Connecticut Yankee in King Arthur's Court (1889).

The couple's marriage lasted 34 years until Olivia's death in 1904. All of the Clemens family are buried in Elmira's Woodlawn Cemetery.

Love of science and technology

Twain was fascinated with science and scientific inquiry. He developed a close and lasting friendship with Nikola Tesla, and the two spent much time together in Tesla's laboratory.

Twain patented three inventions, including an "Improvement in Adjustable and Detachable Straps for Garments" (to replace suspenders) and a history trivia game. Most commercially successful was a self-pasting scrapbook; a dried adhesive on the pages needed only to be moistened before use. Over 25,000 were sold.

Twain was an early proponent of fingerprinting as a forensic technique, featuring it in a tall tale in Life on the Mississippi (1883) and as a central plot element in the novel Pudd'nhead Wilson (1894).

Twain's novel A Connecticut Yankee in King Arthur's Court (1889) features a time traveler from the contemporary U.S., using his knowledge of science to introduce modern technology to Arthurian England. This type of historical manipulation became a trope of speculative fiction as alternate histories.

In 1909, Thomas Edison visited Twain at his home in Redding, Connecticut and filmed him. Part of the footage was used in The Prince and the Pauper (1909), a two-reel short film. It is the only known existing film footage of Twain.

Financial troubles

Twain made a substantial amount of money through his writing, but he lost a great deal through investments. He invested mostly in new inventions and technology, particularly the Paige typesetting machine. It was a beautifully engineered mechanical marvel that amazed viewers when it worked, but it was prone to breakdowns. Twain spent $300,000 (equal to $9,000,000 in inflation-adjusted terms) on it between 1880 and 1894, but before it could be perfected it was rendered obsolete by the Linotype. He lost the bulk of his book profits, as well as a substantial portion of his wife's inheritance.

Twain also lost money through his publishing house, Charles L. Webster and Company, which enjoyed initial success selling the memoirs of Ulysses S. Grant but failed soon afterward, losing money on a biography of Pope Leo XIII. Fewer than 200 copies were sold.

Twain and his family closed down their expensive Hartford home in response to the dwindling income and moved to Europe in June 1891. William M. Laffan of The New York Sun and the McClure Newspaper Syndicate offered him the publication of a series of six European letters. Twain, Olivia, and their daughter Susy were all faced with health problems, and they believed that it would be of benefit to visit European baths. The family stayed mainly in France, Germany, and Italy until May 1895, with longer spells at Berlin (winter 1891/92), Florence (fall and winter 1892/93), and Paris (winters and springs 1893/94 and 1894/95). During that period, Twain returned four times to New York due to his enduring business troubles. He took "a cheap room" in September 1893 at $1.50 per day (equivalent to $42 in 2018) at The Players Club, which he had to keep until March 1894; meanwhile, he became "the Belle of New York," in the words of biographer Albert Bigelow Paine.

Twain's writings and lectures enabled him to recover financially, combined with the help of his friend, Henry Huttleston Rogers. He began a friendship with the financier in 1893, a principal of Standard Oil, that lasted the remainder of his life. Rogers first made him file for bankruptcy in April 1894, then had him transfer the copyrights on his written works to his wife to prevent creditors from gaining possession of them. Finally, Rogers took absolute charge of Twain's money until all his creditors were paid.

Twain accepted an offer from Robert Sparrow Smythe and embarked on a year-long, around the world lecture tour in July 1895 to pay off his creditors in full, although he was no longer under any legal obligation to do so. It was a long, arduous journey and he was sick much of the time, mostly from a cold and a carbuncle. The first part of the itinerary took him across northern America to British Columbia, Canada, until the second half of August. For the second part, he sailed across the Pacific Ocean. His scheduled lecture in Honolulu, Hawaii had to be canceled due to a cholera epidemic. Twain went on to Fiji, Australia, New Zealand, Sri Lanka, India, Mauritius, and South Africa. His three months in India became the centerpiece of his 712-page book Following the Equator. In the second half of July 1896, he sailed back to England, completing his circumnavigation of the world begun 14 months before.

Twain and his family spent four more years in Europe, mainly in England and Austria (October 1897 to May 1899), with longer spells in London and Vienna. Clara had wished to study the piano under Theodor Leschetizky in Vienna. However, Jean's health did not benefit from consulting with specialists in Vienna, the "City of Doctors". The family moved to London in spring 1899, following a lead by Poultney Bigelow who had a good experience being treated by Dr. Jonas Henrik Kellgren, a Swedish osteopathic practitioner in Belgravia. They were persuaded to spend the summer at Kellgren's sanatorium by the lake in the Swedish village of Sanna. Coming back in fall, they continued the treatment in London, until Twain was convinced by lengthy inquiries in America that similar osteopathic expertise was available there.

In mid-1900, he was the guest of newspaper proprietor Hugh Gilzean-Reid at Dollis Hill House, located on the north side of London. Twain wrote that he had "never seen any place that was so satisfactorily situated, with its noble trees and stretch of country, and everything that went to make life delightful, and all within a biscuit's throw of the metropolis of the world." He then returned to America in October 1900, having earned enough to pay off his debts. In winter 1900/01, he became his country's most prominent opponent of imperialism, raising the issue in his speeches, interviews, and writings. In January 1901, he began serving as vice-president of the Anti-Imperialist League of New York.

Speaking engagements

Twain was in great demand as a featured speaker, performing solo humorous talks similar to modern stand-up comedy. He gave paid talks to many men's clubs, including the Authors' Club, Beefsteak Club, Vagabonds, White Friars, and Monday Evening Club of Hartford.

In the late 1890s, he spoke to the Savage Club in London and was elected an honorary member. He was told that only three men had been so honored, including the Prince of Wales, and he replied: "Well, it must make the Prince feel mighty fine." He visited Melbourne and Sydney in 1895 as part of a world lecture tour. In 1897, he spoke to the Concordia Press Club in Vienna as a special guest, following the diplomat Charlemagne Tower, Jr. He delivered the speech "Die Schrecken der Deutschen Sprache" ("The Horrors of the German Language")—in German—to the great amusement of the audience. In 1901, he was invited to speak at Princeton University's Cliosophic Literary Society, where he was made an honorary member.

Canadian visits

In 1881, Twain was honored at a banquet in Montreal, Canada where he made reference to securing a copyright. In 1883, he paid a brief visit to Ottawa, and he visited Toronto twice in 1884 and 1885 on a reading tour with George Washington Cable, known as the "Twins of Genius" tour.

The reason for the Toronto visits was to secure Canadian and British copyrights for his upcoming book Adventures of Huckleberry Finn, to which he had alluded in his Montreal visit. The reason for the Ottawa visit had been to secure Canadian and British copyrights for Life on the Mississippi. Publishers in Toronto had printed unauthorized editions of his books at the time, before an international copyright agreement was established in 1891. These were sold in the United States as well as in Canada, depriving him of royalties. He estimated that Belford Brothers' edition of The Adventures of Tom Sawyer alone had cost him ten thousand dollars (equivalent to $280,000 in 2018). He had unsuccessfully attempted to secure the rights for The Prince and the Pauper in 1881, in conjunction with his Montreal trip. Eventually, he received legal advice to register a copyright in Canada (for both Canada and Britain) prior to publishing in the United States, which would restrain the Canadian publishers from printing a version when the American edition was published. There was a requirement that a copyright be registered to a Canadian resident; he addressed this by his short visits to the country.

Later life and death

... the report is greatly exaggerated.

—Twain's reaction to a report of his death

Twain lived in his later years at 14 West 10th Street in Manhattan. He passed through a period of deep depression which began in 1896 when his daughter Susy died of meningitis. Olivia's death in 1904 and Jean's on December 24, 1909, deepened his gloom. On May 20, 1909, his close friend Henry Rogers died suddenly. In 1906, Twain began his autobiography in the North American Review. In April, he heard that his friend Ina Coolbrith had lost nearly all that she owned in the 1906 San Francisco earthquake, and he volunteered a few autographed portrait photographs to be sold for her benefit. To further aid Coolbrith, George Wharton James visited Twain in New York and arranged for a new portrait session. He was resistant initially, but he eventually admitted that four of the resulting images were the finest ones ever taken of him.

Twain formed a club in 1906 for girls whom he viewed as surrogate granddaughters called the Angel Fish and Aquarium Club. The dozen or so members ranged in age from 10 to 16. He exchanged letters with his "Angel Fish" girls and invited them to concerts and the theatre and to play games. Twain wrote in 1908 that the club was his "life's chief delight". In 1907, he met Dorothy Quick (aged 11) on a transatlantic crossing, beginning "a friendship that was to last until the very day of his death".

Oxford University awarded Twain an honorary doctorate in letters in 1907.

Twain was born two weeks after Halley's Comet's closest approach in 1835; he said in 1909:

I came in with Halley's Comet in 1835. It is coming again next year, and I expect to go out with it. It will be the greatest disappointment of my life if

I don't go out with Halley's Comet. The Almighty has said, no doubt: "Now here are these two unaccountable freaks; they came in together, they must go out together".

Twain's prediction was accurate; he died of a heart attack on April 21, 1910, in Redding, Connecticut, one day after the comet's closest approach to Earth.

Upon hearing of Twain's death, President William Howard Taft said:

Mark Twain gave pleasure – real intellectual enjoyment – to millions, and his works will continue to give such pleasure to millions yet to come ... His humor was American, but he was nearly as much appreciated by Englishmen and people of other countries as by his own countrymen. He has made an enduring part of American literature.

Twain's funeral was at the Brick Presbyterian Church on Fifth Avenue, New York. He is buried in his wife's family plot at Woodlawn Cemetery in Elmira, New York. The Langdon family plot is marked by a 12-foot monument (two fathoms, or "mark twain") placed there by his surviving daughter Clara. There is also a smaller headstone. He expressed a preference for cremation (for example, in Life on the Mississippi), but he acknowledged that his surviving family would have the last word.

Officials in Connecticut and New York estimated the value of Twain's estate at $471,000 ($13,000,000 today).

Writing

Overview

Twain began his career writing light, humorous verse, but he became a chronicler of the vanities, hypocrisies, and murderous acts of mankind. At mid-career, he combined rich humor, sturdy narrative, and social criticism in Huckleberry Finn. He was a master of rendering colloquial speech and helped to create and popularize a distinctive American literature built on American themes and language.

Many of his works have been suppressed at times for various reasons. The

Adventures of Huckleberry Finn has been repeatedly restricted in American high schools, not least for its frequent use of the word "nigger", which was in common usage in the pre-Civil War period in which the novel was set.

A complete bibliography of Twain's works is nearly impossible to compile because of the vast number of pieces he wrote (often in obscure newspapers) and his use of several different pen names. Additionally, a large portion of his speeches and lectures have been lost or were not recorded; thus, the compilation of Twain's works is an ongoing process. Researchers rediscovered published material as recently as 1995 and 2015.

Early journalism and travelogues

Twain was writing for the Virginia City newspaper the Territorial Enterprise in 1863 when he met lawyer Tom Fitch, editor of the competing newspaper Virginia Daily Union and known as the "silver-tongued orator of the Pacific". He credited Fitch with giving him his "first really profitable lesson" in writing. "When I first began to lecture, and in my earlier writings," Twain later commented, "my sole idea was to make comic capital out of everything I saw and heard." In 1866, he presented his lecture on the Sandwich Islands to a crowd in Washoe City, Nevada. Afterwards, Fitch told him:

Clemens, your lecture was magnificent. It was eloquent, moving, sincere. Never in my entire life have I listened to such a magnificent piece of descriptive narration. But you committed one unpardonable sin – the unpardonable sin. It is a sin you must never commit again. You closed a most eloquent description, by which you had keyed your audience up to a pitch of the intensest interest, with a piece of atrocious anti-climax which nullified all the really fine effect you had produced.

It was in these days that Twain became a writer of the Sagebrush School; he was known later as its most famous member. His first important work was "The Celebrated Jumping Frog of Calaveras County," published in the New York Saturday Press on November 18, 1865. After a burst of popularity, the Sacramento Union commissioned him to write letters about his travel experiences. The first journey that he took for this job was to ride the steamer Ajax on its maiden voyage to the Sandwich Islands (Hawaii).

All the while, he was writing letters to the newspaper that were meant for publishing, chronicling his experiences with humor. These letters proved to be the genesis to his work with the San Francisco Alta California newspaper, which designated him a traveling correspondent for a trip from San Francisco to New York City via the Panama isthmus.

On June 8, 1867, he set sail on the pleasure cruiser Quaker City for five months, and this trip resulted in The Innocents Abroad or The New Pilgrims' Progress. In 1872, he published his second piece of travel literature, Roughing It, as an account of his journey from Missouri to Nevada, his subsequent life in the American West, and his visit to Hawaii. The book lampoons American and Western society in the same way that Innocents critiqued the various countries of Europe and the Middle East. His next work was The Gilded Age: A Tale of Today, his first attempt at writing a novel. The book, written with his neighbor Charles Dudley Warner, is also his only collaboration.

Twain's next work drew on his experiences on the Mississippi River. Old Times on the Mississippi was a series of sketches published in the Atlantic Monthly in 1875 featuring his disillusionment with Romanticism. Old Times eventually became the starting point for Life on the Mississippi.

Tom Sawyer and Huckleberry Finn

Twain's next major publication was The Adventures of Tom Sawyer, which draws on his youth in Hannibal. Tom Sawyer was modeled on Twain as a child, with traces of schoolmates John Briggs and Will Bowen. The book also introduces Huckleberry Finn in a supporting role, based on Twain's boyhood friend Tom Blankenship.

The Prince and the Pauper was not as well received, despite a storyline that is common in film and literature today. The book tells the story of two boys born on the same day who are physically identical, acting as a social commentary as the prince and pauper switch places. Twain had started Adventures of Huckleberry Finn (which he consistently had problems completing) and had completed his travel book A Tramp Abroad, which describes his travels through central and southern Europe.

Twain's next major published work was the Adventures of Huckleberry Finn, which confirmed him as a noteworthy American writer. Some have called it the first Great American Novel, and the book has become required reading in many schools throughout the United States. Huckleberry Finn was an offshoot from Tom Sawyer and had a more serious tone than its predecessor. Four hundred manuscript pages were written in mid-1876, right after the publication of Tom Sawyer. The last fifth of Huckleberry Finn is subject to much controversy. Some say that Twain experienced a "failure of nerve," as critic Leo Marx puts it. Ernest Hemingway once said of Huckleberry Finn:

If you read it, you must stop where the Nigger Jim is stolen from the boys. That is the real end. The rest is just cheating.

Hemingway also wrote in the same essay:

All modern American literature comes from one book by Mark Twain called Huckleberry Finn.

Near the completion of Huckleberry Finn, Twain wrote Life on the Mississippi, which is said to have heavily influenced the novel. The travel work recounts Twain's memories and new experiences after a 22-year absence from the Mississippi River. In it, he also explains that "Mark Twain" was the call made when the boat was in safe water, indicating a depth of two fathoms (12 feet or 3.7 metres).

Later writing

Twain produced President Ulysses S. Grant's Memoirs through his fledgling publishing house, Charles L. Webster & Company, which he co-owned with Charles L. Webster, his nephew by marriage.

At this time he also wrote "The Private History of a Campaign That Failed" for The Century Magazine. This piece detailed his two-week stint in a Confederate militia during the Civil War. He next focused on A Connecticut Yankee in King Arthur's Court, written with the same historical fiction style as The Prince and the Pauper. A Connecticut Yankee showed the absurdities of political and social norms by setting them in the court of King Arthur. The book was started in December 1885, then shelved a few months later until the summer of 1887, and eventually finished in the spring of 1889.

His next large-scale work was Pudd'nhead Wilson, which he wrote rapidly, as he was desperately trying to stave off bankruptcy. From November 12 to December 14, 1893, Twain wrote 60,000 words for the novel. Critics[who?] have pointed to this rushed completion as the cause of the novel's rough organization and constant disruption of the plot. This novel also contains the tale of two boys born on the same day who switch positions in life, like The Prince and the Pauper. It was first published serially in Century Magazine and, when it was finally published in book form, Pudd'nhead Wilson appeared as the main title; however, the "subtitles" make the entire title read: The Tragedy of Pudd'nhead Wilson and the Comedy of The Extraordinary Twins.

Twain's next venture was a work of straight fiction that he called Personal Recollections of Joan of Arc and dedicated to his wife. He had long said[where?] that this was the work that he was most proud of, despite the criticism that he received for it. The book had been a dream of his since childhood, and he claimed that he had found a manuscript detailing the life of Joan of Arc when he was an adolescent. This was another piece that he was convinced would save his publishing company. His financial adviser Henry Huttleston Rogers quashed that idea and got Twain out of that business altogether, but the book was published nonetheless.[citation needed]

To pay the bills and keep his business projects afloat, Twain had begun to write articles and commentary furiously, with diminishing returns, but it was not enough. He filed for bankruptcy in 1894. During this time of dire financial straits, he published several literary reviews in newspapers to help make ends meet. He famously derided James Fenimore Cooper in his article detailing Cooper's "Literary Offenses". He became an extremely outspoken critic of other authors and other critics; he suggested that, before praising Cooper's work, Thomas Lounsbury, Brander Matthews, and Wilkie Collins "ought to have read some of it".

George Eliot, Jane Austen, and Robert Louis Stevenson also fell under Twain's attack during this time period, beginning around 1890 and continuing until his death. He outlines what he considers to be "quality writing" in several letters and essays, in addition to providing a source for the "tooth and claw" style of literary criticism. He places emphasis on concision, utility of word choice, and realism; he complains, for example, that Cooper's Deerslayer purports to be realistic but has several shortcomings. Ironically, several of his own works were later criticized for lack of continuity (Adventures of Huckleberry Finn) and organization (Pudd'nhead Wilson).

Twain's wife died in 1904 while the couple were staying at the Villa di Quarto in Florence. After some time had passed he published some works that his wife, his de facto editor and censor throughout her married life, had looked down upon. The Mysterious Stranger is perhaps the best known, depicting various visits of Satan to earth. This particular work was not published in Twain's lifetime. His manuscripts included three versions, written between 1897 and 1905: the so-called Hannibal, Eseldorf, and Print Shop versions. The resulting confusion led to extensive publication of a jumbled version, and only recently have the original versions become available as Twain wrote them.

Twain's last work was his autobiography, which he dictated and thought would be most entertaining if he went off on whims and tangents in non-chronological order. Some archivists and compilers have rearranged the biography into a more conventional form, thereby eliminating some of Twain's humor and the flow of the book. The first volume of the autobiography, over 736 pages, was published by the University of California in November 2010, 100 years after his death, as Twain wished. It soon became an unexpected best-seller, making Twain one of a very few authors publishing new best-selling volumes in the 19th, 20th, and 21st centuries.

Censorship

Twain's works have been subjected to censorship efforts. According to Stuart (2013), "Leading these banning campaigns, generally, were religious organizations or individuals in positions of influence – not so much working librarians, who had been instilled with that American "library spirit" which honored intellectual freedom (within bounds of course)". In 1905, the Brooklyn Public Library banned both The Adventures of Huckleberry Finn and The Adventures of Tom Sawyer from the children's department because of their language.

Views

Twain's views became more radical as he grew older. In a letter to friend and fellow writer William Dean Howells in 1887 he acknowledged that his views had changed and developed over his lifetime, referring to one of his favorite works:

When I finished Carlyle's French Revolution in 1871, I was a Girondin; every time I have read it since, I have read it differently – being influenced and changed, little by little, by life and environment ... and now I lay the book down once more, and recognize that I am a Sansculotte! And not a pale, characterless Sansculotte, but a Marat.

Anti-imperialist

Before 1899, Twain was an ardent imperialist. In the late 1860s and early 1870s, he spoke out strongly in favor of American interests in the Hawaiian Islands. He said the war with Spain in 1898 was "the worthiest" war ever fought. In 1899, however, he reversed course. In the New York Herald, October 16, 1900, Twain describes his transformation and political awakening, in the context of the Philippine–American War, to anti-imperialism:

I wanted the American eagle to go screaming into the Pacific ... Why not spread its wings over the Philippines, I asked myself? ... I said to myself, Here are a people who have suffered for three centuries. We can make them as free as ourselves, give them a government and country of their own, put a miniature of the American Constitution afloat in the Pacific, start a brand new republic to take its place among the free nations of the world. It seemed to me a great task to which we had addressed ourselves.

But I have thought some more, since then, and I have read carefully the treaty of Paris [which ended the Spanish–American War], and I have seen that we do not intend to free, but to subjugate the people of the Philippines. We have gone there to conquer, not to redeem.

It should, it seems to me, be our pleasure and duty to make those people free, and let them deal with their own domestic questions in their own way. And so I am an anti-imperialist. I am opposed to having the eagle put its talons on any other land.

During the Boxer rebellion, Twain said that "the Boxer is a patriot. He loves his country better than he does the countries of other people. I wish him success."

From 1901, soon after his return from Europe, until his death in 1910, Twain was vice-president of the American Anti-Imperialist League, which opposed the annexation of the Philippines by the United States and had "tens of thousands of members". He wrote many political pamphlets for the organization. The Incident in the Philippines, posthumously published in 1924, was in response to the Moro Crater Massacre, in which six hundred Moros were killed. Many of his neglected and previously uncollected writings on anti-imperialism appeared for the first time in book form in 1992.

Twain was critical of imperialism in other countries as well. In Following the Equator, Twain expresses "hatred and condemnation of imperialism of all stripes". He was highly critical of European imperialists, such as Cecil Rhodes, who greatly expanded the British Empire, and Leopold II, King of the Belgians. King Leopold's Soliloquy is a stinging political satire about his private colony, the Congo Free State. Reports of outrageous exploitation and grotesque abuses led to widespread international protest in the early 1900s, arguably the first large-scale human rights movement. In the soliloquy, the King argues that bringing Christianity to the country outweighs a little starvation. Leopold's rubber gatherers were tortured, maimed and slaughtered until the movement forced Brussels to call a halt.

During the Philippine–American War, Twain wrote a short pacifist story titled The War Prayer, which makes the point that humanism and Christianity's preaching of love are incompatible with the conduct of war. It was submitted to Harper's Bazaar for publication, but on March 22, 1905, the magazine rejected the story as "not quite suited to a woman's magazine". Eight days later, Twain wrote to his friend Daniel Carter Beard, to whom he had read the story, "I don't think the prayer will be published in my time. None but the dead are permitted to tell the truth." Because he had an exclusive contract with Harper & Brothers, Twain could not publish The War Prayer elsewhere; it remained unpublished until 1923. It was republished as campaigning material by Vietnam War protesters.

Twain acknowledged that he had originally sympathized with the more moderate Girondins of the French Revolution and then shifted his sympathies to the more radical Sansculottes, indeed identifying himself as "a Marat" and writing that the Reign of Terror paled in comparison to the older terrors that preceded it. Twain supported the revolutionaries in Russia against the reformists, arguing that the Tsar must be got rid of by violent means, because peaceful ones would not work. He summed up his views of revolutions in the following statement:

I am said to be a revolutionist in my sympathies, by birth, by breeding and by principle. I am always on the side of the revolutionists, because there never was a revolution unless there were some oppressive and intolerable conditions against which to revolute.

Civil rights

Twain was an adamant supporter of the abolition of slavery and the emancipation of slaves, even going so far as to say, "Lincoln's Proclamation ... not only set the black slaves free, but set the white man free also". He argued that non-whites did not receive justice in the United States, once saying, "I have seen Chinamen abused and maltreated in all the mean, cowardly ways possible to the invention of a degraded nature ... but I never saw a Chinaman righted in a court of justice for wrongs thus done to him". He paid for at least one black person to attend Yale Law School and for another black person to attend a southern university to become a minister.

Twain's sympathetic views on race were not reflected in his early writings on American Indians. Of them, Twain wrote in 1870:

His heart is a cesspool of falsehood, of treachery, and of low and devilish instincts. With him, gratitude is an unknown emotion; and when one does him a kindness, it is safest to keep the face toward him, lest the reward be an arrow in the back. To accept of a favor from him is to assume a debt which you can never repay to his satisfaction, though you bankrupt yourself trying. The scum of the earth!

As counterpoint, Twain's essay on "The Literary Offenses of Fenimore Cooper" offers a much kinder view of Indians. "No, other Indians would have noticed these things, but Cooper's Indians never notice anything. Cooper thinks they are marvelous creatures for noticing, but he was almost always in error about his Indians. There was seldom a sane one among them." In his later travelogue Following the Equator (1897), Twain observes that in colonized lands all over the world, "savages" have always been wronged by "whites" in the most merciless ways, such as "robbery, humiliation, and slow, slow murder, through poverty and the white man's whiskey"; his conclusion is that "there are many humorous things in this world; among them the white man's notion that he is less savage than the other savages". In an expression that captures his East Indian experiences, he wrote, "So far as I am able to judge nothing has been left undone, either by man or Nature, to make India the most extraordinary country that the sun visits on his rounds. Where every prospect pleases, and only man is vile."

Twain was also a staunch supporter of women's rights and an active campaigner for women's suffrage. His "Votes for Women" speech, in which he pressed for the granting of voting rights to women, is considered one of the most famous in history.

Helen Keller benefited from Twain's support as she pursued her college education and publishing despite her disabilities and financial limitations. The two were friends for roughly 16 years.

Through Twain's efforts, the Connecticut legislature voted a pension for Prudence Crandall, since 1995 Connecticut's official heroine, for her efforts towards the education of African-American young ladies in Connecticut. Twain also offered to purchase for her use her former house in Canterbury, home of the Canterbury Female Boarding School, but she declined.

Labor

Twain wrote glowingly about unions in the river boating industry in Life on the Mississippi, which was read in union halls decades later. He supported the labor movement, especially one of the most important unions, the Knights of Labor. In a speech to them, he said:

Who are the oppressors? The few: the King, the capitalist, and a handful of other overseers and superintendents. Who are the oppressed? The many: the nations of the earth; the valuable personages; the workers; they that make the bread that the soft-handed and idle eat.

Religion

Twain was a Presbyterian. He was critical of organized religion and certain elements of Christianity through his later life. He wrote, for example, "Faith is believing what you know ain't so", and "If Christ were here now there is one thing he would not be – a Christian". With anti-Catholic sentiment rampant in 19th century America, Twain noted he was "educated to enmity toward everything that is Catholic". As an adult, he engaged in religious discussions and attended services, his theology developing as he wrestled with the deaths of loved ones and with his own mortality.

Twain generally avoided publishing his most controversial opinions on religion in his lifetime, and they are known from essays and stories that were published later. In the essay Three Statements of the Eighties in the 1880s, Twain stated that he believed in an almighty God, but not in any messages, revelations, holy scriptures such as the Bible, Providence, or retribution in the afterlife. He did state that "the goodness, the justice, and the mercy of God are manifested in His works", but also that "the universe is governed by strict and immutable laws", which determine "small matters", such as who dies in a pestilence. At other times, he wrote or spoke in ways that contradicted a strict deist view, for example, plainly professing a belief in Providence. In some later writings in the 1890s, he was less optimistic about the goodness of God, observing that "if our Maker is all-powerful for good or evil, He is not in His right mind". At other times, he conjectured sardonically that perhaps God had created the world with all its tortures for some purpose of His own, but was otherwise indifferent to humanity, which was too petty and insignificant to deserve His attention anyway.

In 1901, Twain criticized the actions of the missionary Dr. William Scott Ament (1851–1909) because Ament and other missionaries had collected indemnities from Chinese subjects in the aftermath of the Boxer Uprising of 1900. Twain's response to hearing of Ament's methods was published in the North American Review in February 1901: To the Person Sitting in Darkness, and deals with examples of imperialism in China, South Africa, and with the U.S. occupation of the Philippines. A subsequent article, "To My Missionary Critics" published in The North American Review in April 1901, unapologetically continues his attack, but with the focus shifted from Ament to his missionary superiors, the American Board of Commissioners for Foreign Missions.

After his death, Twain's family suppressed some of his work that was especially irreverent toward conventional religion, including Letters from the Earth, which was not published until his daughter Clara reversed her position in 1962 in response to Soviet propaganda about the withholding. The anti-religious The Mysterious Stranger was published in 1916. Little Bessie, a story ridiculing Christianity, was first published in the 1972 collection Mark Twain's Fables of Man.

He raised money to build a Presbyterian Church in Nevada in 1864.

Twain created a reverent portrayal of Joan of Arc, a subject over which he had obsessed for forty years, studied for a dozen years and spent two years writing about. In 1900 and again in 1908 he stated, "I like Joan of Arc best of all my books, it is the best".

Those who knew Twain well late in life recount that he dwelt on the subject of the afterlife, his daughter Clara saying: "Sometimes he believed death ended everything, but most of the time he felt sure of a life beyond."

Twain's frankest views on religion appeared in his final work Autobiography of Mark Twain, the publication of which started in November 2010, 100 years after his death. In it, he said:

There is one notable thing about our Christianity: bad, bloody, merciless, money-grabbing, and predatory as it is – in our country particularly and in all other Christian countries in a somewhat modified degree – it is still a hundred times better than the Christianity of the Bible, with its prodigious crime – the invention of Hell. Measured by our Christianity of to-day, bad as it is, hypocritical as it is, empty and hollow as it is, neither the Deity nor his Son is a Christian, nor qualified for that moderately high place. Ours is a terrible religion. The fleets of the world could swim in spacious comfort in the innocent blood it has spilled.

Twain was a Freemason. He belonged to Polar Star Lodge No. 79 A.F.&A.M., based in St. Louis. He was initiated an Entered Apprentice on May 22, 1861, passed to the degree of Fellow Craft on June 12, and raised to the degree of Master Mason on July 10.

Twain visited Salt Lake City for two days and met there members of The Church of Jesus Christ of Latter-day Saints. They also gave him a Book of Mormon. He later wrote in Roughing It about that book:

The book seems to be merely a prosy detail of imaginary history, with the Old Testament for a model; followed by a tedious plagiarism of the New Testament.

Vivisection

Twain was opposed to the vivisection practices of his day. His objection was not on a scientific basis but rather an ethical one. He specifically cited the pain caused to the animal as his basis of his opposition:

I am not interested to know whether Vivisection produces results that are profitable to the human race or doesn't. ... The pains which it inflicts upon unconsenting animals is the basis of my enmity towards it, and it is to me sufficient justification of the enmity without looking further.

Pen names

Twain used different pen names before deciding on "Mark Twain". He signed humorous and imaginative sketches as "Josh" until 1863. Additionally, he used the pen name "Thomas Jefferson Snodgrass" for a series of humorous letters.

He maintained that his primary pen name came from his years working on Mississippi riverboats, where two fathoms, a depth indicating water safe for the passage of boat, was a measure on the sounding line. Twain is an archaic term for "two", as in "The veil of the temple was rent in twain." The riverboatman's cry was "mark twain" or, more fully, "by the mark twain", meaning "according to the mark [on the line], [the depth is] two [fathoms]", that is, "The water is 12 feet (3.7 m) deep and it is safe to pass."

Twain said that his famous pen name was not entirely his invention. In Life on the Mississippi, he wrote:

Captain Isaiah Sellers was not of literary turn or capacity, but he used to jot down brief paragraphs of plain practical information about the river, and sign them "MARK TWAIN", and give them to the New Orleans Picayune. They related to the stage and condition of the river, and were accurate and valuable; ... At the time that the telegraph brought the news of his death, I was on the Pacific coast. I was a fresh new journalist, and needed a nom de guerre; so I confiscated the ancient mariner's discarded one, and have done my best to make it remain what it was in his hands – a sign and symbol and warrant that whatever is found in its company may be gambled on as being the petrified truth; how I have succeeded, it would not be modest in me to say.

Twain's story about his pen name has been questioned by some with the suggestion that "mark twain" refers to a running bar tab that Twain would regularly incur while drinking at John Piper's saloon in Virginia City, Nevada. Samuel Clemens himself responded to this suggestion by saying, "Mark Twain was the nom de plume of one Captain Isaiah Sellers, who used to write river news over it for the New Orleans Picayune. He died in 1869 and as he could no longer need that signature, I laid violent hands upon it without asking permission of the proprietor's remains. That is the history of the nom de plume I bear."

In his autobiography, Twain writes further of Captain Sellers' use of "Mark Twain":

I was a cub pilot on the Mississippi River then, and one day I wrote a rude and crude satire which was leveled at Captain Isaiah Sellers, the oldest steamboat pilot on the Mississippi River, and the most respected, esteemed, and revered. For many years he had occasionally written brief paragraphs concerning the river and the changes which it had undergone under his observation during fifty years, and had signed these paragraphs "Mark Twain" and published them in the St. Louis and New Orleans journals. In my satire I made rude game of his reminiscences. It was a shabby poor performance, but I didn't know it, and the pilots didn't know it. The pilots thought it was brilliant. They were jealous of Sellers, because when the gray-heads among them pleased their vanity by detailing in the hearing of the younger craftsmen marvels which they had seen in the long ago on the river, Sellers was always likely to step in at the psychological moment and snuff them out with wonders of his own which made their small marvels look pale and sick. However, I have told all about this in "Old Times on the Mississippi." The pilots handed my extravagant satire to a river reporter, and it was published in the New Orleans True Delta. That poor old Captain Sellers was deeply wounded. He had never been held up to ridicule before; he was sensitive, and he never got over the hurt which I had wantonly and stupidly inflicted upon his dignity. I was proud of my performance for a while, and considered it quite wonderful, but I have changed my opinion of it long ago. Sellers never published another paragraph nor ever used his nom de guerre again.

Legacy and depictions

Trademark white suit

While Twain is often depicted wearing a white suit, modern representations suggesting that he wore them throughout his life are unfounded. Evidence suggests that Twain began wearing white suits on the lecture circuit, after the death of his wife Olivia ("Livy") in 1904. However, there is also evidence showing him wearing a white suit before 1904. In 1882, he sent a photograph of himself in a white suit to 18-year-old Edward W. Bok, later publisher of the Ladies Home Journal, with a handwritten dated note. The white suit did eventually become his trademark, as illustrated in anecdotes about this eccentricity (such as the time he wore a white summer suit to a Congressional hearing during the winter). McMasters' The Mark Twain Encyclopedia states that Twain did not wear a white suit in his last three years, except at one banquet speech.

In his autobiography, Twain writes of his early experiments with wearing white out-of-season:

Next after fine colors, I like plain white. One of my sorrows, when the summer ends, is that I must put off my cheery and comfortable white clothes and enter for the winter into the depressing captivity of the shapeless and degrading black ones. It is mid-October now, and the weather is growing cold up here in the New Hampshire hills, but it will not succeed in freezing me out of these white garments, for here the neighbors are few, and it is only of crowds that I am afraid. (Source: Wikipedia)

CPSIA information can be obtained
at www.ICGtesting.com
Printed in the USA
LVHW111211140420
653275LV00013BA/316

9 789389 682038